My Rainbow

by Trinity and DeShanna Neal
illustrated by Art Twink

Kokila

Kokila

An imprint of Penguin Random House LLC, New York

Text copyright © 2020 by DeShanna Neal
Illustrations copyright © 2020 by Art Twink

Kokila with colophon is a registered trademark of Penguin Random House LLC.

Visit us online at penguinrandomhouse.com

Library of Congress Cataloging-in-Publication Data is available.

Printed in China
ISBN 9781984814609

1 3 5 7 9 10 8 6 4 2

Design by Jasmin Rubero
Text set in Boucherie Flared

The art for this book was created digitally.

To grandpop, the one who loved me and my rainbow.
I'll miss you.
—T. N. and D. N.

Thank you to all Black women, who make the world a more
beautiful place to live.
—A. T.

Trinity and her siblings played in the warm morning sunlight.

Trinity stroked Peter Porker's long mane. She *loved* soft things, just like many kids with autism, and Peter's hair was *perfect*.

Music sang from Lucien's cello, enveloping the room in tranquility and making it feel safe.

"Let's play, Trin!" Hyperion said. Their sparkly shirt glittered like stars.

Sometimes Trinity and Hyperion's dolls were video gamers. Sometimes they were astronauts. Little Thane's toy was a hot dog this time. Their dolls could be anything, just like Mom said they could!

Trinity stayed with her doll long after everyone found other things to do. She stared at its long, curly hair and beautiful dark skin. She touched her own short hair.

"What's the matter, baby?" Mom asked.

Trinity blew out a gust of breath in frustration. "I can't be a girl."

"Oh?" Mom said. "Why is that?"

"Because."

"Because *why*?"

Trinity glanced up. "I need long hair."

"Girls can have short hair. See?" Mom ran a hand over her short black hair. "I'm a girl, too."

Trinity's frown only deepened. "I don't think you understand, Mom. I'm a transgender girl."

Mom blinked with surprise. Trinity's gender was part of what made her a masterpiece, just like her autism and her Black skin. But Trinity was trying to tell her something important.

Mom closed her laptop and sat down next to Trinity. "I'm listening."

Trinity let out a *big* breath, as if she'd been holding it forever. "People don't care if cisgender girls like you have short hair. But it's different for transgender girls. I *need* long hair!"

Mom thought for a long moment.
"You're right. It is different for me."

She peered at each of her children. "We are all a little different from one another. You're a beautiful rainbow, Trinity."

"I don't feel like a rainbow right now."

Mom knew Trinity struggled to grow her hair long. She hated how it made her itchy when it was growing out. But Trinity knew herself best of all. And if she said she needed long hair, she NEEDED long hair! With a sigh, Trinity picked up a pink comb and began smoothing her doll's hair.

When Dad came home from work, Mom was still thinking about what Trinity had said. "I have to make things right," Mom said. "But *how*?"

"I don't know," Dad said.

Mom didn't know, either.

Lucien peeked around the corner. "I think I can help."

Mom grabbed her purse. Lucien led her across the street to the beauty store. There were *so many choices*!

"That one's too long," Lucien said. "Trinity doesn't like hair touching her neck."

"And that one's too straight," Mom said next. "She's a beautiful Black girl and her curly hair is *already* perfect. None of these feel right." She sighed.

Lucien thought hard. "I know what we need."

That night, as all her children slept, Mom sat down with her laptop, a hair needle, thread, and a wig cap. She had never made a wig before. She threaded the hair into the cap like the online videos showed. She sewed late into the night, weaving love into every row.

The wig had to be *just right* for Trinity. She poked herself with the needle a few times, got the thread tangled in the curls, and had to chase Peter when he snatched a strand of curly purple hair.

But she weaved and weaved until the clock struck three a.m.

She finally dozed off, hoping her daughter would love it.
Mom awoke to the sound of sniffling.
And sobbing.
She gasped. Trinity was crying!

Mom dashed to the bathroom. The wig was big and fluffy on Trinity's head. The springy, curly teal blue, dark pink, and purple hair that Lucien had chosen lit up the whole room.

Trinity's eyes sparkled. She was crying tears of joy!
She ran her fingers through the curls.

"It's me, Mom.
My hair has finally come!
It's *my* rainbow!"

Lucien bounded into the bathroom, with the rest of the family behind him, to see Trinity's reaction.

"Thank you," Trinity said.

"I love my rainbow."

"And we love you,
my heart."